# *God bless* *my* RUDEBOY

*freestyling*

KRISTOPHER SMITH

authorHOUSE®

*AuthorHouse™*
*1663 Liberty Drive*
*Bloomington, IN 47403*
*www.authorhouse.com*
*Phone: 1-800-839-8640*



*First published by AuthorHouse 01/21/2012*

*ISBN: 978-1-4670-7103-1 (sc)*
*ISBN: 978-1-4670-7102-4 (ebk)*

*Printed in the United States of America*



*This book is printed on acid-free paper.*

# CHAPTER 1

## Shamrock's Point of View

Ever since I was a kid, I wanted to be a dope boy. Growing up in the hood, the dope boys were the neighborhood role models. They always stayed fresh with the cleanest gear. They had nice rides and all the honeys. Growing up in Crenshaw's Projects, the dope boys were legends to us young whippersnappers. It was another Friday night in Crenshaw's Projects, or "The Shaw," as most of us young folk called it. My little brother Kix was just finishing tightening up my fade. Kix could cut a pretty good fade.

He cut hair of half the dudes who lived in the Shaw. He charged five dollars a head, so he also made a little change, too. Instead of me going to a regular barbershop, I'd just let him do it. After he finished, I handed him a ten-dollar bill.

"Since I gave you ten dollars, my next cut is free, right?"

"Whatever," he replied jokingly, as he walked out of my room. I was about to step out for the night. My homeboys and I were supposed to be hitting up Lakeside Strip.

Lakeside Strip was a strip in my city that stretched almost a quarter mile. A lot of young people from all around the city would just come park their vehicles and just chill out. Every weekend it would be jam-packed. I grabbed my nine-millimeter from under my bed, as well as my little stash of dope and my Atlanta Brave's fitted cap from on top of my dresser, and headed out of the front door down the hallway. In my nineteen years on this earth, I've seen a lot of stuff go down in these hallways. I've seen so many fights I can't even remember all of them.

I've seen two brothers who were friends with my older brother Terrance, who's now locked up for second-degree murder, stab each other to death over a female. A kid with whom I went to junior high, named Jarvis, took a nine-millimeter and blew his head off when he found out that he'd contracted HIV. I got so many stories that I could write a book. These hallways in my building definitely had their recollections.

When I got to the end of the hallway, I saw a group of kids around the age of twelve freestyling at the end of the stairway. Freestyle battles were constant in these hallways. A bunch of people would gather round and just rap from off the top of their heads—no rehearsed lines or anything. These freestyle sessions would usually last for hours. By the time the freestyle sessions were over, so many cuss words would have been said that it'd make you want to go home and pick up your Bible. Usually I would've stopped to listen, but I was in a hurry that night. I made my way past them and out of the exit doors.

The Shaw was definitely packed that night. There were at least 100 people outside. Cars were everywhere blasting their music. There were young people arguing, shooting dice, smoking weed, and of course selling dope.

"What's up, Shamrock?" one of my homeboys who lived in the next building yelled.

I threw up at him the deuces, which was what people in my neighborhood called the peace sign. My name was Antron Harris, but my nickname was Shamrock, like the four-leaf clover. I got the nickname because I'd been shooting craps since I was a kid. And I've won a lot of money, so people call me lucky. That's how Shamrock came into play.

"Dang! Where are these dudes?" I said to myself. They were supposed to be picking me up.

"Hey, Shamrock, do you have anything for me today?" a familiar voice yelled from behind me. I turned around. It was Bill, one of the Shaw's biggest fiends. Bill was what everybody called him. I didn't even know if that was his real name. He was about thirty-five years old, but from his face, you'd think he was 150 years old. Bill's face was jacked up. All his teeth in the front row were missing. His clothes looked like they hadn't been washed in years, and he smelled like urine.

Bill was your typical fiend. I'd sell Bill at least two rocks a day. Where he'd get the money to buy them, I didn't know. I'd never seen him with a job since I'd known him, but to be honest, I could not have cared less. As long as he kept putting money in my pocket, I was happy.

"What's up, Bill?" I said as I walked over to him. I abstained from giving him a handshake because you never know where a fiend's hand has been. I sold him his usual stash, and he was off. I stared at him as he walked off and shook my head in pity at him.

I know, I sold dope, but nothing in this world could have made me try the stuff. Bill was a perfect example of what crack could do. It frightened me. I did not want to end up like Bill when I got older. My cell phone vibrated in my pocket. I took it out and read the text message on it. It was from my homey Sno-Cone telling me that they were in the parking lot. I walked over to the parking lot.

I spotted them immediately. Sno-Cone's bright yellow Caprice stuck out like a sore thumb. "It's about time y'all dudes get here," I yelled. I walked up to the car and opened the passenger-side door. My homey Doodle was sitting in the front seat. "So what's up? Are you going to give up the shotgun or what?" I said, asking for the front seat.

Doodle hopped out of the front seat and got into the backseat with my homeboy Milky-Way and some other cat whom I'd never seen before.

"Why are y'all so late?" I asked Sno-Cone as I closed the door.

"Sorry about that, bro. My baby momma was tripping again over random stuff, as usual."

I turned up the volume on the CD player; one of my favorite songs was playing, Prince's "When Dove's Cry." I looked in the rear-view mirror at Doodle. "Doodle, so what's up? Are you going to drop thirty points tonight, or what?" I asked. "I got money riding on this game."

"Homey, with the way that I'm feeling, I might just drop forty points tonight." I could tell by Doodle's composure and his speech that he was high, or as we say in Georgia, "geeked up." Doodle was the city's local basketball star. He played for Caddo Heights High, my old high school. I'd graduated the year before. He was graduating that year, in like two and a half months. He was always getting high. If it hadn't been for basketball, he'd probably never have gone to school.

That was the only reason why all of his teachers were passing him: He was the star on the school's basketball team. He got his nickname Doodle because, when he was a little, his parents said that he kind of resembled a rooster—hence, the name Doodle, short for cock-a-doodle-doo. Every time Doodle would score a basket at one of his games, the whole gym would yell, "Cock-a-doodle-doo." It was the way they honored him. I thought that was pretty cool. He even had a picture of a rooster tattooed on his neck. It was the championship game that night. Our team had been ranked the underdog at the beginning of the playoffs, but we proved everybody wrong.

Still looking in the rear-view mirror, I glanced at the guy sitting next to Doodle, whom I'd never seen before, and as if Sno-Cone was reading my mind or something, he introduced us to each other. "Hey, Shamrock, that's my old friend Ras who's in the backseat. Ras and I go way back. We used to play basketball together in Junior High when I lived in North Carolina. His family moved to Georgia a year after mine did." I turned around and gave him a handshake. I didn't know if I was tripping or what, but as soon as I shook his hand, I automatically got a bad feeling about this dude. He smiled at me; all of his teeth in the front row were gold.

Sno-Cone was the oldest out of all of us. He was like two years older than me. His older brother Daytron and my older brother were friends. That was how we'd met.

I glanced at Milky-Way, who as usual was brushing his nice hair. Milky-Way didn't really hang out with us that much because he went to Moorehouse College. He'd just started his freshman year a couple of months ago. He was one of the smartest brothers whom I knew and also the most conceited. Milky-Way was what you would call a pretty boy.

The dude was a handsome brother, but I'd never tell him that. He was light skinned and about six-foot-four, just a little taller than me. He was sort of built. He was the only brother whom I knew who had green eyes. He modeled part-time. He'd done a couple of men's clothing ads. His only problem was that he'd gotten told by females that he was handsome so many times that he's cockier than a farmhouse rooster. The dude was always brushing his hair. He had nice hair, not like the average black person; it was curlier, most likely because his dad was Puerto Rican. He also stayed on the phone texting women. Milky-Way had a lot of female friends. He was also the only brother I knew who got pedicures and manicures.

I admit—I guess, in a female-ish sort of way—I was kind of jealous of him. "Milky-Way, why are you always brushing your hair? No matter how many times you brush it, you're still going to be ugly," I semi-jokingly said.

"Shamrock, why are you always hating on me?" he replied. "I guess if I had nappy hair like you, though, I hate on me, too," he said jokingly. Everybody in the car burst out laughing.

I admit his remark sort of angered me, since what he said was kind of true. Who was I kidding? It was true. I shot back. "Well, at least I'm not the hood's first metrosexual." Everybody burst out laughing in the car. Milky-Way even chuckled. This was how it would be when the four of us would hang out, cracking jokes on each other and chilling out. This was the crew, Milky-Way, Doodle, Sno-Cone, and me. I've pretty much described everyone's attributes, with the exception of me.

By the time we arrived at the school's parking lot, it was jam-packed. A lot of people had shown up. "I bet there's a lot of females up in the gym," Milky-Way said.

"Dude, why are you always talking about females?" I said, feeling aggravated.

"Because I'm a pimp," he replied.

"Yeah whatever, bro," I replied. "Hey, Sno-Cone, can I stick my piece under your car seat, because you know Caddo Heights still has those raggedly metal detectors at the front entrance?" I asked.

"Yeah, go ahead, man."

I pulled out my nine-millimeter, which I had tucked in the back of my red monkey jeans, and placed it under the passenger-side seat. We walked inside the gym, and just like I predicted, the two metal detectors that were there for all of my four years at Caddo Heights were still there at the front entrance.

We passed through them and made our way to the gymnasium. The gym was packed. Caddo Heights had a huge gym, so there were at least 600 people inside of it. J Kwon's Hood hop was playing. The cheerleaders were sitting down on the sidelines.

One of the cheerleaders was my homegirl Keisha Martin—one of the prettiest girls I'd ever seen. Keisha was light skinned because she was black mixed with Puerto Rican. She had long hair, and she wore braces. Every time that she smiled, it's like the sun just had came out. She sort of resembled the 1980s singer Pebbles. Keish, which was what I called her for short, was scheduled to graduate with Doodle in two months. She saw me looking at her and waved. I stuck my hand by my ear, signaling for her to call me as soon as she got home.

I started my way up the bleachers, but as soon as I started to make my way up them, someone tapped me on the back. I turned around. It was CJ. He was also on the school's basketball team. He was the point guard. Last year when I was a senior, we used to battle him before every game. What I mean by battle is the two of us would have a dance-off right there inside of the gym in front of everybody. An impromptu dance-off—the crowd always loved it. It was sort of like hype before the game. I'd always win. CJ had some pretty good moves, but he wasn't any match for me. I was known as a dancer in the Shaw. Everybody knew that I could move.

I'd won a billion talent shows in school, too. I could also sing. Before my mom passed away from breast cancer, I was in our church's choir. I'd sung solo a few times, as well. After my mom passed away though, I'd stop going to church. I hadn't sung in a while, except for maybe in the shower or something. CJ pointed toward the Caddo Heights cheerleading team. The deejay put on the song "Grinding" by The Clipse. The crowd saw what was about to happen and started to get riled up. CJ started to do a combination of slides on the floor. His moves were impressive. He'd have given Chris Brown and Usher a run for their money.

The audience loved him. After he was finished, I told the deejay to put on the song "Yeah" by Usher. I started off my routine doing the bucking dance. Bucking was a dance move that consisted of slides and a lot of arm movements. A lot of people who lived in the Memphis area were known to do it. People in Georgia weren't hip to it, so I knew that the dance that I was doing was new to probably half of the people there. I could tell most of them were impressed by my moves. Even CJ was staring in awe. I finished off my dance routine with a backward flip. The crowd erupted with cheers. CJ and I always got as much attention as the basketball games. After I was finished, CJ and I gave each other a handshake. I went to go take my seat. I took a seat by Sno-Cone.

"That was hot, man," he said, complimenting me.

The tipoff began. Doodle's team won the tipoff. CJ passed Doodle the ball. He dribbled to the foul line and put up a jump shot. The shot sank through the basket. Everybody in the crowd chanted cock-a-doodle-doo. I could tell this was going to be a good game.

# Chapter 2

## Alaina's Point of View

It was 7:50 PM. In ten more minutes, I'd be getting off of my job at Edge Me Ups barbershop. All I had to do was clean up the hair from around my station, and I'd be finished. I'd been working at Edge Me Ups for almost a month and a half then. Edge Me Ups was my city's biggest urban barbershop. I was the only female out of the twenty employees who worked there. In my opinion I was one of the best hairstylists who worked there, but by my lack of clientele, you'd think otherwise. About 90 percent of the customers who came into Edge Me Ups were guys, and most guys where I'm from would rather a guy to cut their hair, rather than a girl. My business was pretty low compared to the other employees.

The other 10 percent were women, and only 6 percent of those customers were mine because women aren't biased as much as men are when it comes to getting their hair fixed. A lot of men hairstylists can do women's hair just as good as a woman, and sometimes even better. I'd been styling hair ever since I was ten. I started out styling all of my aunts' and sisters' hair; then all of the elder ladies who stayed on my street heard how good I was, and they started letting me fix their hair.

After I finished sweeping up all of the hair from around my station, I grabbed my jacket and purse and left the shop. It was a nice spring night in Georgia. Since it was such a nice night, and I only lived twenty minutes away, I decided to walk home. My brother Rashawn would usually pick me up from work. I took my Sidekick cell phone from out of my purse and texted him, telling him I would be walking home that night. Georgia's streets were busy at that time. It was a Friday night, and young people were rushing home, trying to get ready for the weekend. I was thinking about maybe going to go see a movie or something. I heard that there was a new movie playing that night with my favorite actor of all time starring in it, Allen Payne.

I considered asking my two best friends Candy and Brandy if they would like to go. I lived on Dean Street, with my older sister LaNeisha and my younger sister Vanessa. I'd stayed on this street since I was about ten. I was twenty-one. My family and I used to live in North Carolina, but my mother and father died in a terrible car accident, of which I was a part. From there, my older sister LaNeisha, my older brother Rashawn, my younger sister Vanessa, and I moved all the way down to Georgia with my Aunt Kay.

My older brother and sister eventually moved out and got jobs. Vanessa and I moved in with my older sister LaNeisha. Rashawn didn't come around much, except to drop off his son—my adorable little nephew, Terrance—for Vanessa and or me to babysit. Most of the time Rashawn was in the streets. Rashawn was into the streets very hard. He sold drugs, carried guns, and the whole nine yards. Three of his cars had been shot up. It really hurt me that Rashawn was into that type of lifestyle. Before Mom and Dad died, he and I were very close, but he never came around.

LaNeisha and he didn't get along with each other well, mainly because LaNeisha was a church-going woman and wouldn't tolerate his reckless behavior. Vanessa was too young to care; she loved him though. I still saw him as my big brother Rashawn. When he'd come around, he'd always ask me how everything had been going.

I finally turned onto my street. "Home sweet home," I whispered. My block was crowded with cars and people. That was usual for a Friday night. The stench of marijuana smoke filled the night's air. Cars and loud music filled the streets. There were at least 75 to 125 people out on the streets.

Even though I lived there, I didn't associate with too many people on the block. I know that sort of sounds anti-social, but I am a homebody kind of girl. LaNeisha was always telling me the Bible said you should love thy neighbor, and I had a lot of neighbors. My two best friends Candy and Brandy, who were twins, stayed like two blocks away from me. They'd been my friends since I moved. After about a dozen catcalls and guys asking me for my number, I'd finally made it to my house. "I'm home," I yelled.

I went into my bedroom, which I shared with my younger sister Vanessa. Vanessa was sixteen. Vanessa and I had shared the same room ever since the first day we both moved in with LaNeisha. In a couple of months though, if business picked up at the shop, I was planning to get my own place. As much as I wanted my own pad though, I would miss sharing a room with Vanessa. Vanessa was plopped down on her canopy bed, chatting on the cordless about some guy.

"What's up, big head?" I said to her. That had been my nickname for her ever since she was six. I always joked with her about having a big head, even though she was beautiful.

"Hey, Alaina," she replied. I began to get out of my clothes, so that I could jump into the showers "Hey, Alaina, there's a dance coming up at school. Can you help me with my hair?"

"Yeah, I'll see what I can do."

"What about my homegirl, Teesha?"

"Yes, Vanessa, just tell her to come over this weekend." I went into the bathroom and showered. After I finished showering, I put on a polo shirt, apple bottom jeans, and some of my favorite perfume, White Diamond by Liz Taylor. I put on a crispy new pair of Air Force Ones. Surprisingly, Vanessa was finished talking on the telephone. I grabbed it, plopped down on my canopy bed, and began to call Candy and Brandy.

The phone rang three times, and Candy picked it up. "What's up, Candy? Do y'all wanna hit up a movie tonight?"

"You know I do. Let me ask this lazy sister of mine if she wants to go." There was a pause on the phone for a couple of seconds, and then she came back. "Brandy says that she's down to roll. We'll be by to pick you up in like twenty minutes."

"Aight," I replied and hung up. I looked at my watch; it was 9:40. I went to my dresser drawer and pulled out my old photo album.

I flipped it to a page of my mother and father hugging under an oak tree. The picture was taken before I was born. They looked so young and happy back then. My momma was so pretty. My parents died in a car wreck when I was six. I can remember the horrible accident as if it was yesterday. Before the accident, my family and I lived in North Carolina. We were coming back from a trip of seeing my grandparents, who lived Raleigh. It was only my parents and me.

I was sitting in the backseat being mischievous, as always when I rode on those long, boring road trips to visit my grandparents. My dad had just finished scolding me for some reason, and I didn't like the tone of voice that he'd used on me. So I threw my teddy bear into the front seat. My dad took his eye off the road for a couple of seconds to turn around to scold me, and when he did, our car just barely went into the other lane. An oncoming car nudged it, and we flew out of control and flipped over two times. To make a long story short, my parents were instantly killed, and I survived.

The accident traumatized me a great deal. After the accident, our Aunt Kay took us in, and that's where my troubles began. From there on, I blamed myself as being the cause of the death of my parents. I started getting flashbacks of the accident. I could be sitting at the table eating, and I'd get a flashback and start panicking. I'd get them during homeroom in school and sometimes choir practice at church. I'd have nightmares, too. The flashbacks would usually last for about twenty-five seconds. My grades started to drop in school, and I became depressed. Aunt Kay sent me to a psychiatrist by the name of Tina Collins, and I went to her every Thursday for the next fourteen years.

I still held myself responsible for my parents' death. It was a guilt that I thought that I'd never get over. Everyone told me that it's not my fault—that I was only a child and didn't know any better—but I refused to listen. If my dad hadn't have turned around to scold me, my parents would still be alive today. What guilt to have on my tiny little shoulders.

The telephone rang, and I picked it up. It was Candy. "Hey, Brandy was just telling me about this championship basketball game that our old school was having against some school in Lakeside. Do you want to go to it instead of the movies?"

"Isn't Lakeside where all the gangsters and thugs live? It's more dangerous than where we live," I replied.

"Girl, why do you have to be so scared all the time?" she replied. "I promise that we'll be alright."

I thought about it. "Alright, but nothing stupid better go down tonight."

"I can't believe that I let you two drag me here," I said as we pulled on Lakeside Strip and parked. The strip was crowded that night. There were cars everywhere. People were sitting on the hoods of their car, with some even standing on top of their hoods. It was wild. Everybody had decided to go to Lakeside Strip after the game. From the jump, I thought it was a bad idea, but Candy and Brandy outnumbered me—plus, it was their car.

"That game was incredible," Brandy said.

"Yeah, it's just too bad that we lost," I replied as I suspiciously scoped out our surroundings from the backseat.

"That cute light-skinned brother the home crowd was cheering for named Doodle was amazing. He had like forty points, and he hit the game-winning three-pointer at the buzzer," Candy said.

"He was handsome, too," Brandy added.

"He's probably out here amongst this large crowd somewhere," I said.

"Hey, y'all, I'm about to drop the top on this hoopty," Candy said. She unlatched the hook that connected the roof to the car on the driver's side. Brandy disconnected the one on the passenger's side. She then pressed a red button near the CD player, and the car's roof started to descend.

"Yeah, now we have some invisible roof in this joint," Brandy yelled excitedly.

"Hey do y'all want to get out and mingle? There's a lot of our old classmates out here tonight," Candy asked.

They both looked at me. I gave them a look that showed that I was annoyed. "Whatever," I replied.

We got out of the car and began to walk. I was a little scared being there in Lakeside Strip. I had all the reason to be. Lakeside Strip constantly was getting aired on the news every weekend for a shooting. It was kind of weird; Candy and Brandy were both five-foot-two and 110 pounds, but they acted like they were giants.

They weren't scared of anything. Our neighborhood was far from a walk in the park. We'd had our share of drive-bys and shootouts, but that didn't seem to faze Candy and Brandy. They'd still sit on their porch at 10:00 at night flirting with some guys on the cordless. They were some very beautiful girls. Their mom was mixed with Cherokee Indian, so they were both light skinned and had long, gorgeous hair. They'd won a lot of beauty pageants in their day.

Sometimes I didn't like to hang out with them because I felt out of place. I mean, I didn't consider myself an ugly girl. My hair was almost as long as theirs, and people said that I resembled Ashanti, the singer—but I admit I didn't feel as pretty or confident as them. Guys were already gawking at them as we were walking. Suddenly, a loud thunderous growl out of nowhere startled me. Two guys in front of us were instigating their two dogs to fight one another. One was a huge pit bull, and the other was a stocky Rottweiler. We eased past them.

"Hey, isn't that y'all hero over there?" I said as I pointed forward. It was Doodle, the hoop star. He was leaning against a yellow Caprice and standing next to one of the most beautiful guys that I'd ever seen in my life. He was tall, light skinned, and handsome. His hair was curly. His teeth were pearly white. The only other people whom I'd seen with teeth as white as his were Candy and Brandy.

There were like seven to ten girls standing around them like they were celebrities or something. We decided to introduce ourselves. We walked up to the crowd. Doodle and his handsome friend noticed Candy and Brandy, and their eyes lit up. Candy and Brandy walked toward them, and the crowd sort of parted for them.

"What y'all name is, Shawty?" Doodle asked in his thick Georgian accent. Shawty was what most of the young folk called each other in Georgia.

"Hi, I'm Brandy, and this is my sister Candy." Brandy started to look around for me. I kind of fell into the crowd of girls around them. She grabbed my arm and pulled me beside them. "This is our best friend Alaina."

"How are y'all doing?" I said shyly.

"Three beautiful women," Doodle's handsome friend said.

"Well, I'm Doodle, and this is my friend Milky-Way."

"Twins," Milky-Way replied. "Y'all looked so nice—God had to make y'all images twice."

Candy blushed. "That was sweet," Brandy replied.

"That was a pretty impressive game, Doodle. You really put the hurting on my old high school tonight," I said.

"Thanks, Shawty. I figured that I'd show out tonight."

"You're going to have to teach me that jump shot of yours sometimes," Brandy said flirtingly.

"Well, just give me your number, and we can get together sometime," he answered. He pulled out his Blackberry and began to type Brandy's number into it.

I glanced over at Candy. She and Doodle were smiling and flirting with each other. You see, just like that, Candy and Brandy made friends. Seeing Doodle and Milky-Way tied up, all the other girls began to scatter. I sort of went unnoticed. I noticed a crowd beginning to form not too far from where we were standing. At first, I thought a fight was about to break out and quickly got worried, but I heard cheers instead of arguing. I cautiously walked over to the crowd.

There were two guys in the middle of the circle dancing to a Three Six Mafia song, a rap group I used to listen to when I was younger. They were both sliding across the concrete pavement. The dancer with the Atlanta Braves fitted cap caught my attention. He danced slightly better than the other guy. He had some gorgeous eyes. I liked his moves. They danced until the song was over. The crowd died down.

I decided to go up and introduce myself to him. I walked up to him and extended my hand. "That was some great dancing," I told him.

"Thanks," he replied and smiled. He looked at my shoes.

"Those are some nice kicks that you're wearing. I saw you at the game wearing them."

"Oh thanks," I replied. I looked at his haircut. Being a barber, I always observed people's hairstyles. "You have a nice lineup. Who does your hair?"

He blushed. I thought the dimples on his cheeks were cute. "Thank you. My little brother Kix cut it. Cutting hair is sort of his talent."

"Well, it's mine also, and your brother is very good."

I reached into my pocket, pulled out my business card, and gave to him. "Stop by my shop sometime, and let me line you up."

He took the card and looked at it. "Alaina, the master stylist. I might just have to pay you a visit," he said. We both stood there smiling at each other.

"You know there's something so familiar about your eyes," I said.

"What's that?"

"Well, you kind of . . ." My sentence was cut off when suddenly, out of nowhere, five gunshots rang through the midnight air. Everybody started dispersing. The guy and I both ran our separate ways.

I ran to Candy and Brandy's car. They were already inside of it. Candy cranked up the car and sped off. Oh, what a night! "I planned on going to the movies and ended up running for my life," I thought. The handsome dancer that I met still lingered in my mind. I didn't even get his name.

"Momma and Daddy get up!" I yelled. "Somebody help! Please somebody help!" I tossed and turned in my bed. LaNeisha and Vanessa came and shook me to snap me out of my nightmare. I awoke crying.

LaNeisha put my head upon her chest. "It's alright, Alaina. We're here, baby." She semi-cradled me while Vanessa rubbed my hair. I lay there sobbing. I had another one of my nightmares. It was three in the morning. This was a normal thing for this household. I'd have one of my episodes, and LaNeisha and Vanessa would rush in and calm me down. What a night! First the shootings and now this—I probably was going to call in sick for work.

# CHAPTER 3

## Ras's Point of View

"It is hot as an oven in here," I thought as I waited in that wash-eteria. I was there with my boy Sno-Cone to pick up his homeboy Shamrock. Shamrock worked here as a coin exchanger, the person to whom the customers gave coins in exchange for quarters. I kind of got the feeling, though, that this was sort of a front to throw the police off. I had a good feeling that Shamrock was selling dope out of here. He probably had an agreement with the owner in exchange for a cut.

I glanced at the white man in front of the glass window that Shamrock worked behind. It was very rare to see a middle-aged white man in Lakeside. He probably drove that shiny white Lexus outside that was parked next to Sno-Cones's car. It was very obvious what type of transaction was going down. I watched the man as he walked outside and hopped into the Lexus. Just like I suspected . . . this was what we called a "dope spot." The reason why I knew so much about this business was because I used to slang dope, but soon I had workers like Shamrock slanging it for me. I was one of my block's most successful dope connects. I wasn't a kingpin or anything like that, but if it was crack, cocaine, weed, or whatever, I had it. I'd been pushing dope for like ten years, and I was twenty-four—about to turn twenty-five in like two months.

Lately though I'd been thinking of just getting out of the dope game. I was getting too old for all the drama that came with the business. I'd been shot at numerous of times. I'd been shot in my arm twice. I'd been kidnapped, and I'd even kidnapped people. Plus, I had a son to look after. I wanted to stick around to see him grow older.

Terrill and Shamrock came from behind the window and walked toward the exit. "It's about time," I mumbled. I rose out of my seat. I gave Shamrock a head nod as to tell him, "What's up?" He looked at me and ignored me.

That was very disrespectful. Shamrock had been acting funny toward me ever since the first night that I met him in Sno-Cone's car. If it was anyone else other than my homeboy's homeboy, I would've stepped to him, but it was my friend's friend—so I was going to let him breathe. I sort of thought that he was jealous of Sno-Cones's friendship with me.

I didn't know why I was hanging out with these little kids anyway. I was like four or five years older than both of them. It was already bad enough that they were from Lakeside. I never hung out in Lakeside. I'm not a scared guy or anything, but cats who stayed over here were crazy. Lakeside was ranked the year before with the third highest murder rate in the country. My part of town had a high crime rate, too, but not as bad as Lakeside. I was actually scared to drive through some neighborhoods over there.

The three of us walked outside. I opened the passenger-side door and hopped in. "Hey, homey, I always ride shotgun," Shamrock said to me.

"Well, you won't be riding in the passenger seat today, homeboy," I replied.

"Well, we ain't leaving this parking lot until I get in the front seat."

"Hey, Ras, just give up the front seat to keep down confusion," Sno-Cone said.

I restrained myself from doing or saying anything bad that would ruin my relationship with Sno-Cone and got out of the car and into the backseat. These young dudes were really starting to push my buttons. We drove off.

"Hey, dog, can you swing by Keisha's house for a second? Today's her birthday, and I want to give her a birthday present."

"What did you get her?" Sno-Cone asked.

Shamrock held up a wad of money. "Nothing says, 'Happy Birthday,' like money," he replied.

"I don't get it, Shamrock. You two have known each other since y'all were kids, and y'all have never gone out. Why is that?"

"Man, Keish is my homegirl. Before Kix and I moved with Aunt Jesse, she stayed next door to us. When our momma would get all strung out on heroine and start beating on me, I used to go to her bedroom window, and she'd always sneak me in and let me sleep in her room until the next morning."

"Did you ever try to a move on her?"

"Nope. We've kissed a couple of times, but nothing more than that."

"Didn't you say her brother hates you or something?"

"Yeah, her older knucklehead brother Tazarus—he can't stand me. He's in a gang, too."

"Has he ever stepped to you?"

"No, we've had words with each other but nothing serious."

"Dang, bro! Your situation sounds like the ghetto version of Romeo and Juliet."

We drove for about five minutes, and then we pulled into Sommer's Projects. I observed the graffiti written on the buildings. Most of it was all gang related. We pulled into a parking space. There was a group of men between the ages of nineteen and twenty-eight standing by a 1964 Impala. I could tell that they were all in a gang because all of them were wearing red bandannas on their wrist or around their neck.

"Man, I knew I shouldn't have come over here with these Lakeside dudes," I thought. We got out of the car.

"Hey, Shamrock, hurry up and do what you got to do because I'm a little uncomfortable being over here," Sno-Cone said.

"Man, stop being so scared," he replied.

Some of them began to walk over to us. "Hey, who y'all is?" one of them yelled to us. I was starting to get a little nervous.

"Hey, is your sister here, dog?" Shamrock asked one of them.

He was wearing a white undershirt with a red bandanna tied around his neck. He was the biggest person in the group. "Yeah, she's here, but I'm the only one who asks the questions around here. Now, I know who these two little knuckleheads are, but who are you?" He came and stood in front of me. I instantly got a little nervous.

"I'm Ras, homey," I replied.

"Are you a blood?" he asked, grimacing in my face.

"No, I don't gang bang, homey."

"First off, I'm not your homey. Suwoo!" he yelled. Even though I wasn't in a gang I knew what "suwoo" meant. He was calling all of his crew. His crew that was standing by the 1964 Impala started walking toward us. "Hey, folk, we have an outsider amongst us." They all began to look at me.

# Chapter 4
## Shamrock's Point of View

Keisha was sure looking pretty. She had her hair let down, similar to the way the late R&B singer Aaliyah wore hers back in the day. I gave her a hug. "Happy Birthday, Keish." I pinned the wad of money on her shirt. She'd already had a lot of twenty- and fifty-dollar bills pinned on her—most likely given to her by all of her other guy friends.

"Thank you, Shamrock."

"So what do you want to do tonight?" I asked. "Are you going to Chucky Cheese, like we used to back in the day?" I asked jokingly.

She laughed. "Well, my friend Semaj is taking me out to dinner tonight, and then we are probably going to hit up the movies or something."

I looked at her like I was hurt. "Oh, so you can hang out with Semaj, but you don't want to kick it with me."

"Shamrock don't even front because you know I'll hang out with you over anyone else. But Semaj asked me last month to take me out on my birthday."

"Well, the brother sounds desperate to me." I replied.

She laughed. "Well, changing subjects, have you thought about what we talked about on the phone two weeks ago?"

"Two weeks ago—I can barely remember what I talked about yesterday."

"Oh, so now you have amnesia?" she asked rhetorically. "We talked about you enrolling in college."

I made a face that showed that I was annoyed. "Yeah, I thought about it, but I haven't made any decisions yet."

She then made a face that showed that she was annoyed. "Shamrock, you make me so angry. You have all of this potential, and you won't put it to use. You'd rather run around on these dangerous streets. Do you want to be a dope boy all of your life?"

"Girl, you starting to sound just like my Aunt Jesse." The doorbell rang. "Saved by the bell," I mumbled.

"I heard that," she replied as she went to answer the door. There was a black guy who was about six feet tall standing at it.

He gave Keisha a big hug. Watching them hug sort of made me jealous. "Happy Birthday!" he smiled and said. He noticed the money that was pinned on her shirt and grabbed some money out of his pocket. He pinned four crisp hundred dollars on her.

"Semaj, I want to introduce you to my best friend Shamrock," she said putting emphasis on the word best. "This is my friend Shamrock. Shamrock, this is my friend Semaj."

"What's up, dog?" he replied. I could tell that this brother wasn't from around here by the sound of his accent. No one says "dog."

"What's up, homey?" I replied. "I never seen you around Caddo Heights. When did you graduate?" I asked.

"I didn't go to Caddo Heights. I'm from Savannah, Georgia."

"Savannah," I replied.

"Yeah and I've been out of school, bro, for a while. I'm twenty-four and I'm in college trying to finish up pre-med."

"Did you say you were twenty-four?" I asked. I couldn't believe Keisha was going out with a twenty-four-year-old guy.

"Yeah," he replied. There was an awkward silence.

"Well, I think I better be leaving," I said getting up and walking toward the door.

Keisha came and gave me a hug. "I'm going to call you tonight, alright?" she said

"Aight," I replied. "Hey, homey, show my homegirl a good time now," I told Semaj.

"I will," he replied. I walked out of the apartment feeling kind of jealous. I couldn't believe Keisha was going out with this older brother instead of me.

I looked toward Sno-Cone, and to my surprise, Tazarus and Ras were in each other's faces. I jogged down the stairway to see what was going on.

"Look, homeboy. I ain't no punk, and I ain't one of your little flunkies standing over there," Ras was saying pointing at his crew.

"Man, who are you calling flunkies?" one of the crew members said, stepping toward Ras. All of them began to reach for their guns; Tazarus motioned his crew back.

"Hey, dog, I don't know whether you're slow or just crazy, but I suggest that you be getting out of these neck of the woods."

"Hey, Sno, let's jet, man," I said.

"Yeah, I suggest that y'all do that, and don't bring this dude back over here."

The three of us got into Sno's car. All of their eyes were fixated on us. As we drove out of the parking lot, they threw gang signs at us. I turned around and looked at Ras. "Man, are you stupid or what? You could've gotten us killed! I don't know what y'all be doing in y'all neighborhood, but you don't come to nobody's hood talking smack. This is Lakeside, dog."

"Forget Lakeside," he said.

"Forget what?" I replied. "Do you want to get out of the car and settle this?" I said. I had gotten fed up with Ras, thinking he could just barge in on somebody's crew.

"It ain't nothing but a thing, lil dude," he replied.

"Hey, both of y'all, chill!" Sno-Cone yelled. "Y'all two fight like brothers or something."

"Look, Sno-Cone, just take me home. Whenever you come to pick me up, just make sure he's not in the car with you," I said.

"Yeah, the same goes for me, too, homey," Ras replied.

When Sno-Cone arrived at the Shaw, I got out and walked toward my house without turning my head to say bye. I was so angry that I didn't know what to do. I walked up to my building.

"Hey, Shamrock," a voice yelled from above my head. I looked up. It was Text, one of my homeboys, on the roof. "Hey, dog, come up to the roof. It's about to go down up here."

I made my way up the stairs and unto the roof. The roof was packed. It was always packed. Local gangs would hold meetings up there. There'd be basketball games up there, too. I walked over to my homeboy. "What's up?"

"Man, Tommy Gunz and Bugs from the fourth floor are about to throw down." Tommy Gunz was a cat who lived in the Shaw. I didn't know him too well. All I knew was that he used to be one of the most feared people in the Shaw when I was younger. I'd heard stories about him.

Bugs was another guy in our building with whom I didn't associate as well.

"Why are they fighting?" I asked.

"Man, I don't know. I think they're fighting over an ex-girlfriend or something. All I know is I got fifty bucks that Tommy Gunz whips this dude's butt." I glanced over at Tommy. His shirt was off showing his gigantic muscles. He'd gotten them from being in prison. There were tattoos all over his chest. He had a mean scowl on his face. Tommy Gunz was an imposing creature to look at. I'm not a scared guy, but I'd never agree to fight him.

"Do you want to get in on this bet, Shamrock?"

"No, I'm good." Bugs came busting through the entrance. Bugs was no slouch either. I'd also heard stories about him. He walked up to Tommy and stared into his face. They stared menacingly at each other. I knew that it was about to go down. "Well, Text, I'm about to call it a day, bro."

"You're not going to stick around for the fight?"

"Naw, man, if something go down up here, I ain't trying to see nothing. I don't want to be any witnesses for no cops."

He gave me a pound on the hand. "Alright then, my dude, I'm going to get at you later."

As soon as I walked out, I heard the crowd going crazy. The first hit had been thrown. I'd grown out of watching fights. Before my older brother went to jail, I'd seen him get in a ton of fights.

I went into the house and jumped straight into the shower. When I finished showering,

I went into my bedroom. Kix wasn't there. He was probably out somewhere with his friends. How I wished I had been fourteen again. Kix didn't have a care in this world, except for what his friends thought about him. I kneeled down beside my bed to say my prayers. Even though I hadn't been to church in a while, I said my prayers every night. "Dear God, I want to thank you for allowing me to make it another day. I know there's so many of my friends who aren't here, so I want to thank you.

"I ask you, dear God, to look after my family and friends. I ask you to keep my little brother Kix safe. Don't let him make the mistakes that I've done. I ask you to look after my older brother who's in the pen right now. I also have a problem, God. Lately, my faith has been fading. I've been having trouble determining whether you're real or not.

"It's one part of me that knows you're real, but then there's a part of me that thinks there's no God. I mean, I got friends dying, and I'm selling drugs—my life is in a whirlwind right now. I'm just being real, God. I ask you, God, if you could show me something to let me know that you're real, or am I just destined for destruction? Amen."

I rose from the floor. I heard sirens outside of the building. I went to the window. It looked like all of Atlanta's police had come to the Shaw. My guess was that someone had called the cops on all of them on the roof. "I knew it." I jumped into my bed and fell fast asleep.

# Chapter 5

## Alaina's Point of View

It was Friday evening, and I was just about to finish up my session with my psychiatrist. Ms. Collins, my psychiatrist, was a very attractive lady. She was about in her mid thirties. She had wavy blonde hair and wore short, conservative miniskirts. One time she invited me to hang out with her at the county fair, and the whole day she was getting hit on by a lot of guys. I liked her, but I honestly thought that I wasn't getting anywhere with her.

This was like an ongoing routine. Every time I went to her. She'd ask me the same questions. "Why do you think it's your fault that your parents are dead?" "Why are you so guilty?" And so on. Then I'd say that I didn't know. This Friday evening wasn't any different from the rest.

"Alaina, what I want you to do is to look in the mirror every morning when you get up. Look at yourself and repeat the words, 'I am somebody.' You have to learn to start complimenting yourself, instead of beating yourself up."

"I'll try, but I don't think that it's going to help me." I looked at my watch. My hour was almost up. I arose out of my chair.

"I want you to call me . . . like in four days and tell me how you've been doing."

"Alright, Ms. Collins," I replied. I gave her a hug and exited out of her office. I had borrowed LaNeisha's car. In a couple of hours, I had to drop off Vanessa at a dance she was attending. I cranked up the car and sped home.

# CHAPTER 6

## Shamrock's Point of View

It was a Friday evening, and there I was hiding in the corners of a back alley across the street from Sally's Barbeque, sweating like a slave. In any minute, Ms. Sally would be getting off of her job at Sally's Barbeque. Sally's Barbeque was a spot in Lakeside where everybody went to get some good barbeque, but that day, barbeque was the last thing on my mind.

I'd been robbed two days ago coming out of the wash-eteria, and my connect needed his money. He didn't care whether I got robbed or not; he just wanted his cash. I was waiting on Ms. Sally, a little old black lady about in her early seventies, to get off of her shift. She was the owner of the restaurant. Everybody in town knew that Ms. Sally was wealthy because her restaurant got a lot of business.

I hoped the good Lord would forgive me for what I was about to do. I looked at my watch. It read 4:30. A couple seconds later, Ms. Sally stepped out of the restaurant to walk to her car. "Right on time," I whispered. I pulled the ski mask that I had sitting on my head down over my face. I burst out full speed toward Ms. Sally. I approached her right as she was opening up her driver-side door.

"Give me your purse, old lady." I yanked her purse from under her arm, making her fall to the ground. I ran back down the alley that I was hiding in and jumped over the brick wall in the back of it. I hoped God would forgive me for this one. I'd never robbed an old lady before, but I was desperate. I ran all the way home.

"So, what's up, Kotter? Are you going to sell the shotgun to me for 100 dollars or what?" I asked. I was in a back alley with Kotter, one of my old homeboys from high school. I was trying to buy a shotgun from him for 100 dollars. I gazed at all the weapons in the back of his trunk of his Caprice Classic.

He had at least twenty-five guns in it. "Kotter, I don't mean to be nosy, but I have to ask you, bro. Where did you get all of these guns?"

"Man, I inherited these guns from my Uncle Harris when he died."

"You expect me to believe that man?" I replied.

"Whatever," he replied. "Tell you what, Shamrock; since you're my friend, I'll sell you the gun for 100 dollars and those new Jordans that you are wearing right now. What are you like a size 10?" he asked.

"Man, Kotter, I just bought these shoes two days ago."

"Hey, I'm giving you a just deal: 100 dollars and the shoes. It's my final offer."

I thought about it. I couldn't believe I was getting jipped by this dude. "Alright, it's a deal," I said angrily. "Wait right here," I said. I went to my car to put on a pair of old basketball shoes that I had in the backseat of my aunt's jeep. I took 100 dollars out of my pocket and walked over to his car. I gave him the shoes and the money. He inspected the money as if trying to see was it counterfeit or not.

"Dude, are you kidding me? The cash is legit," I said.

"You can never be too sure these days," he replied.

"Well, could you hurry up? I have to take Kix to a dance."

He grabbed the gun out of the back of his trunk and gave it to me. I inspected it. It looked fairly brand new. "This thing better not jam up either, Kotter."

"Come on, Shamrock. You know I wouldn't swindle you."

"Yeah, but you can never be too sure these days," I said mockingly. I put the gun in the back of my aunt's jeep and left.

"Kix was looking quite handsome," I thought as I observed him sitting in my passenger seat. He had on a baby blue, button-down polo shirt; Polo boots; and Evisu jeans. He smelled of Polo Cologne, and his haircut was perfect. I had to give Kix his just credit; at only fourteen, he had class.

It was nighttime, and we were sitting in front of Walnut Hill's High school, in the front of the parking lot. I was mistaken. I had thought Kix's school was throwing a dance, but Kix was the date of some girl who went to this school. Walnut Hill was located in Russel Grove, a part of town about twenty minutes driving distance from Lakeside. I didn't come here to often. As a matter of fact, I hadn't visited this part of town in at least two years. People who lived over here seemed sort of fake to me. It's like they were trying to be something that they weren't. There were a lot of nice neighborhoods in Russel Grove, but there was also a lot of crime. Russel Grove wasn't poor like Lakeside, but still there was a high crime rate.

It wasn't as high as Lakeside, but it was fairly high. Lakeside had a reason to have a high crime rate. We were poor. Russel Grove had no reason that I could think of to have such a high crime rate. The city was filled with a bunch of middle-class, spoiled kids wanting to be thugs. I wondered how Kix met anyone from over here.

"So, big bro, why have you been keeping secrets from me?" He reached in his pocket, pulled out a card, and threw it in my lap. "I found it in your room."

I picked it up and looked at it. It was the business card that the cute chick gave me at the strip like three weeks ago.

"Have you been scoping out other barbershops? Am I not doing a good job or something?" he asked playfully.

"Man, some chick gave me this," I replied. "You know you will always be my favorite barber."

"I better be," he replied. I gave him a playful push.

"Hey, there's my date right there." He pointed to this pretty girl who was at least eighteen walking toward the entrance of the school.

A lot of people were starting to show up now. Kix stuck his head out of the window and yelled at her, "Hey, Gabriel, wait up."

"Hey, Kix, your date is beautiful," I said astonishingly.

"Yeah, she's a senior," he replied. I glanced at her. She had long hair and a butterscotch complexion. She was also tall, and she was wearing a miniskirt that showed off her legs. "Man, Shamrock, you're staring at my date pretty hard. Hey, get out and I'll introduce you to her." We both got out of the car. I could now hear the music coming from the gymnasium. It was very loud.

I could hear what song was being played: Lil Bow Wow and Omarion's "Let Me Hold You." Crowds of people were entering the gym. The entrance to the gym was packed. We approached Kix's date. They hugged and Kix gave her a light peck on the cheek.

"Gabriel, you are looking nice," he said to her.

"Thank you. You're looking pretty smooth yourself."

"Well, hey, you know," he replied, pretending to brush dirt off of his shoulder. "They looked so good together," I thought. "Hey, Gabriel, I want you to meet my brother Shamrock."

"Nice to meet you," I said, shaking her hand.

"Likewise," she replied. She reached in her purse and pulled out a small digital camera. "Hey, Shamrock, could you take a picture of us?" she asked, handing me the camera.

"No problem."

Kix stood behind her and put his arms around her stomach. "I'm not hugging you too tight, am I?" he asked her jokingly. She laughed. I decided that was a good picture of them with each other. I took the snapshot. They looked at me with surprise.

"Sham, we wasn't ready." Kix said.

"Dog, that was a good picture that I just snapped." They looked at the picture.

"Yeah, it is nice," Gabriel replied. Just then the Slick Rick and Doug E. Fresh song "The Show" came on. "Oh, this is my jam, Kix. Let's go in and dance," Gabriel said.

"Hey, Shamrock, you don't want to come and chill out for a few minutes?" Kix asked.

"No, dog. I got to get back; the game's about to start," I replied.

"Aight then. Well, I'm going to catch a ride back with Gabriel and her cousin."

"Aight." I gave Kix a handshake, and they headed into the gym. "Man, I miss high school." I said aloud. Just then someone caught my eye. "Speak of the devil," I whispered. I spotted Alaina, the girl who had given her business card to me that night at the strip. She was saying good-bye to two girls who were entering the gym with two dudes.

I approached her as she walked from them. "What's up, master barber?" I said to her. She turned around and looked at me. At first, it took like three seconds for her to remember who I was.

"You're the dancer, right?" she replied.

"Yeah, Shamrock," I said.

"What are you doing here? You look a little bit too old to be going to a high school dance," she joked.

"I dropped off my little brother," I replied.

"I dropped off my little sister also," she replied. We both stood there staring at each other in silence. "This girl has some pretty eyes," I thought.

"So what are you about to do now?" I asked.

"Well, I'm probably about to go to this little spot called The Hat. I usually go there every weekend."

"The Hat?" I replied.

"Yeah, it's a nice little spot about fifteen minutes from here. It's just a small little spot where young people who are our age go up on stage and perform poetry and sing or rap."

"It's sort of like a talent showcase?" I asked.

"Yeah," she replied.

"Well, do you mind if I tag along with you? I'm sort of bored out of mind?"

"No, I don't mind at all."

"Cool. I'll follow you there then." We both walked to the parking lot, got into our vehicles, and drove off.

We drove for about ten minutes north of Walnut Hill's High until we pulled into the parking lot of this small club with a sign that read, "The Hat." We both exited our cars. We walked into the club. The bouncer at the door gave us free admission since Alaina was a regular at the club. It was fairly packed inside, and the club was more spacious than what it seemed when looking at it from the outside. We took a seat in the front row. A comedian was on stage. He was picking on people in the audience, and most of his victims were sitting in the front row. His jokes were sort of lame.

I had a feeling Alaina and I would be his next targets. He looked at us. "Look at these two right here," he said drawing attention to the two of us. "Who do you two suppose to be: Beauty and the Hoodlum?" A couple of people in the audience laughed. "Where are the two of you coming from: the courthouse?" I loudly booed him. After he finished with Alaina and me, he went on to his next victim.

"Man, that dude was lame," I said to Alaina.

"Yeah, he was, wasn't he?"

"Hey, how can I get up there?" I asked.

"You have to go sign your name on the roster, but what are you going to do?"

"I'm going to sing," I replied. She looked at me with an expression that said, "Yeah right." "I'm serious. I can sing."

"I'm not doubting you. You just don't look like the type that know how's to sing."

"Oh and how does the type that knows how to sing look?" I asked playfully.

She didn't know how to respond. "I'm sorry. Just go up there and do your thing," she wisely responded.

I walked up to the roster and signed my name.

I would be going on after two more people. I came and sat back down. The next two performances were fairly good. The first act was a male rapper by the name of Chaos, and the second act was a singer by the name of Precious. She sang Aretha Franklin's "Respect." After she finished, the announcer came up on to the stage.

"Well, this next brother goes by the name of Shamrock. Let's give him a healthy handclap, ladies and gentleman." I arose from my seat and went up on stage.

The announcer gave me a smile and a pat on the back, and he left the stage. I stepped to the mic. "Hello, ladies and gentlemen. This song that I'm about to sing is from my favorite movie, *Purple Rain*. My momma used to play this song every night before I went to sleep. It's Prince's 'The Beautiful Ones.'"

The reaction from the audience made me think that no one ever performed the song here before. "This is dedicated to my new friend whom I just met." Alaina blushed. The music came in. "Baby, Baby, Baby, what's it gonna be?" I began to sing.

It had been a while since I sang in front of a lot of people. I used to sing solos at church all the time when I was younger. I was a little nervous but not that much because I knew that I could sing very well. Singing and dancing came naturally to me. I could tell that the crowd was loving it. Most of the women in the audience were snapping their fingers and swaying their heads. The best part in the song was about to come up. It was the break of the song where Prince says the poem. I stepped off stage to do it. I walked to Alaina's table. I took her hand. The break came, and I recited the poem.

*Paint a perfect picture*
*Bring to life a vision in one's mind.*
*The beautiful ones will always smash that picture every time.*

The crowd jumped to their feet and cheered, even though I wasn't finished with the song. I walked back on stage. I ended the song on a high note, and the audience rose to their feet and clapped. The comedian who was heckling Alaina and me was also clapping. After I finished, the announcer stepped unto the stage.

He shook my hand.

"Ladies and gentlemen, never in the history of The Hat has a young man ever brought down the house like this gentleman. This is going to be a tough act to follow." I stepped off stage and walked to our table. Alaina hugged me.

"That was incredible!" she said.

"Thank you," I replied.

"Where did you learn to sing like that?" she asked.

"I used to sing in my church's choir when I was younger."

"Oh, you were in your church's choir?"

"Yeah."

"That's crazy. I'm also in my church's choir. I'm a leading soloist."

"That's what's up," I replied.

She looked into my eyes as if she was trying to figure me out. "Hey, do you wanna ditch this place and go somewhere and talk?" she asked.

"Yeah." We walked out of the club toward the parking lot.

"Hey, you got me into trouble with my little brother?"

She looked at me, feeling confused. "How?"

"He found the business card that you gave me, and now he's thinking that I've been checking out different barbers."

She laughed. "Is your brother scared of competition?"

"I haven't seen too many who cut better than my brother."

"Oh, you haven't," she replied. "Get into your car and follow me." She got into her car.

"You sure are bossy," I joked. We got into our cars and left.

# CHAPTER 7

## Alaina's Point of View

"Are you sure you know what you're doing?" Shamrock asked me cautiously as he sat in my barber's chair at Edge Me Ups. We were the only two in the barbershop.

"Shamrock, relax. You're dealing with a pro." I began to cut his hair.

"Your hands are much softer than Kix's," he said.

"It's that a bad thing?" I asked.

"No, not at all," he replied. Twenty minutes later I shut the clippers off.

"Well, I'm all done." I cranked down the barber's chair, and he got out of it and looked in the mirror. I saw a pleased expression on his face.

"Alaina, you got skills. You're on another level than Kix." I smiled. "Yo, what do I owe you?" He reached into his pocket.

"It's on the house. That beautiful serenade that you sung at The Hat was enough."

He looked at my watch. "You know, it's only 10:30; the night is still young. How about I take you to one of my hangout spots?" he asked me.

"It's not Lakeside Strip, is it?" I asked.

"You don't think the strip is the only place I hang out, do you?" he asked. I didn't answer. "No, it's not the strip. I think that you'd like this place."

"Alright then, let's go," I replied.

"There you go again being bossy."

We drove for about twenty minutes until we pulled into Johnson's Gorge. Johnson's Gorge was a small cliff that overlooked the whole city. You could see the whole city for miles away. The city's teenagers also came here to make out. I hoped Shamrock didn't have anything like that planned in mind. If he tried to pull anything, I was gone. We both got out of our cars. I dropped the top on LaNeisha's car. He walked over to me.

"This is where I come to just chill and think. Mind if we sit?" he asked, motioning to he hood of LaNeisha's car. We sat down. "Isn't this beautiful?" he asked.

"It's very beautiful." I said. Up there, the sky was clear, and you could see the stars. The sky was beautiful. Just then Earth Wind and Fire's song "Would you Mind" played on the radio. "This is one of my favorite songs," I said. I went to turn the radio's volume up. I came and sat back down on the hood.

"So, Shamrock, tell me about yourself. What do you do? What is your story?"

"My story?" he asked.

"Yeah, everyone has a story."

"Well, basically, I've lived in Lakeside all my life. My mother died from breast cancer, and my little brother Kix and I had to move in with our Aunt Jesse. I have an older brother who's been in the pen since I was nine for murder."

"Why did you stop singing in your church's choir?" I asked.

"Well, before my mom died, she used to send Kix and me to church every Sunday. Back then, I was a little knucklehead getting into trouble more than what I do now. So my ma thought getting me into choir would keep me out of trouble, and it did. She didn't want me to end up like my older brother. I got really good at singing. I used to come home and practice singing in the mirror. Pretty soon dancing followed. I ended up getting a solo, and I did good on it. The church started giving me more solo songs to sing. I just remember my mother being so proud of me when I was singing. She'd be the loudest person cheering in the church. I had never seen her like that. I was always used to seeing her upset from when she'd have to come to the police station to pick me up for fighting and stealing. It made me feel good to see my mother proud of me. But, when my mother got cancer, she couldn't come to church as much because she was always at the hospital. Six months later she died, and by then I just stopped going. I just lost all motivation to go. My mom wasn't there to cheer me on, so I stopped going. From there, I turned back to my old ways, and here we are today." He looked at me.

"I'm sorry to hear that about your mother," I said.

"It's alright."

"You and me have so much in common," I said.

"How is that?"

"Well, just like you, my parents died, but from a car wreck. One day my family and I were going on a trip to go see my grandparents, right here in Georgia. Back then, my family and I lived in North Carolina, and I was acting up in the backseat. My dad took his eyes off the road only for a second to scold me, and an eighteen-wheeler hit our car. Miraculously, I lived, but they didn't make it. My siblings and I moved in with our grandparents. My older sister LaNeisha, when she turned eighteen, moved out and got her apartment. My younger sister Vanessa and I moved in with her eventually. My older brother Rashawn did his own thing. LaNeisha and he don't get along because he's into the street life. He doesn't come around too often, except to drop off his son: my handsome nephew Jalen. As a matter of fact, you kind of remind me of . . ."

I was interrupted in mid sentence by his cell phone ranging. It was Keisha. He told her that he would call her back. "I'm sorry about that," he apologized. "Anyways, I've been in and out of therapy every since my mom and pops died. Even though I was a little girl and everybody tells me that it wasn't my fault, I still feel responsible for their deaths. I still have flashbacks and nightmares. I couldn't even attend their funeral because I was so messed up. I've prayed on it, but it seems like God hasn't answered me yet.

"These therapy sessions are costing me a fortune. Every week it's the same ongoing routine. My psychiatrist will ask me why I feel guilty, I'll say that I don't know, and she'll tell me to write down a list of things that should make me feel good about myself. I go to church and all hoping that it will take some of my guilt away, but it hasn't so far." I hung my head in silence.

Shamrock gave me a pat on the back. "It's going to be alright.

"It seems to me like you're doing all of this extra stuff to convince yourself that it wasn't your fault, and it isn't working. Maybe you should tell your parents how you feel."

I looked at him like he was stupid or something. "How can I tell my . . ." I cut off my response in mid sentence because I was starting to grow angry. "Just forget about it. What do you know anyway?"

We sat there in silence for a while. "So what are your views on God?" he asked.

"Well, I believe that we're all kind of like puzzle pieces. We're all down here together so that we can help each other out. I believe God leads certain people to us, and he leads us to certain people so that we can help someone out or someone can help us out." He nodded his head in agreement. "What about you? What are your beliefs?" I asked.

"Well, I compare life to freestyling."

"Freestyling?" I asked. "What you mean, like rapping?" I asked.

"Yeah," he replied.

"Shamrock, you are saying some off-the-wall stuff tonight. How in the world is life like freestyling?"

"Well, you know, when a person's freestyling, he's making stuff up as he goes."

"Yeah, but what does that have to do with God?" I asked.

"Well, I believe our lives are just like leaves in the wind. We're down here floating freely around on earth, and we're making up stuff as we're going. Every day, we unexpectedly bump into strangers. We make new friends, and we learn new things. We discover things and learn about God. I believe God has us down here freestyling, and it's our job to make the best out of life as we're going. I believe fate comes from serendipity."

I was quiet for a few seconds. Shamrock had just made the most perfect analogy I'd ever heard. What he'd just said would stay with me forever. "I get what you're saying," I said. "It's sort of like the two of us. We accidentally bumped into each other again by coincidentally dropping both of our younger siblings at a dance, and by our chance meeting, God willing, we might just become best friends."

"Exactly," he said. "Instead of it being serendipity, it could just be a blessing that we happened to bump into each other."

He looked into my eyes. "You're smart, Alaina."

"Thank you," I said. "So where do you see yourself in the next ten years?" I asked.

"Honestly, I don't know. Hopefully, alive," he replied. "I'm just lost right now."

"Well, a smart guy like you will be okay. You can sing and dance, and your philosophy on life rivals that of a real philosopher."

"Thanks," he replied. For the next hour we sort of just lay on top of the hood of his car gazing at the stars and talking about everything from the president to Dennis Rodman.

We had different opinions on issues that stimulated each of our minds to think. After about an hour of conversing, we exchanged phone numbers, got into our cars, and headed home. When I got home, it was like 12:00. Vanessa had already made it back. I took a shower and got into bed. I couldn't fall asleep at the moment. Shamrock's words were still in my head. "Are we all just freestyling down here for the time being? Could be." I dosed off.

# CHAPTER 8

## Shamrock's Point of View

It was 2:00 in the afternoon when I got the news that would eventually change my life. I'd just come in from shooting basketball with Kix, and as soon as I stepped in, my Aunt Jesse told me that Alaina had called. I admit I had gotten pretty excited when I heard that she had called.

I really had had a good time hanging out with her that night. She was very interesting. I called her from my cell phone. The phone rang three times, and she picked up.

"Hello," she said.

"Hey, what's up? This is Shamrock."

"What's up, Shamrock? I called you today, but your Aunt said you were out playing basketball."

"Yeah, I was out schooling my little brother."

"Well, I got some news for you."

"What type of news?" I asked.

"Well, I told my choir director on the phone today about a new friend that I met. I told him about his amazing singing ability, and he wants my new friend to come in for rehearsal today."

"Hold on. Let me get this straight. You want me to come in today and sing at your church?"

"Yeah."

"Alaina, I haven't been to church in years."

"So? Nobody's going to judge you. I know you're going to blow them all away."

"Alaina, I don't know."

"Man, come on, Shamrock. Do it for me please."

I thought about it. It was going to feel kind of weird being in church. I hadn't stepped foot in a church since my mom died. Alaina was my new homegirl though, and I didn't want to disappoint her. "Alright. I'll go," I said.

"Thank you, Shamrock," she replied. "Come to Alma's drive around six o'clock, and the church will be on the left."

"Alright," I replied. We hung up. I had no idea what I was getting myself into. I went to go take a shower.

It was 5:50 pm, and I was pulling onto Alma's Street. I saw the church on the left, just like she had said. I pulled into the parking lot and parked the car. The church's parking lot was fairly packed. I started to get nervous. "Maybe I shouldn't have come," I thought. I had told Alaina that I was coming though. I decided to go in. I got out of the car and walked into the church. The church was fairly big inside. The majority of everyone was sitting in the pews.

There were mostly older people there. I looked up onto the stage and spotted Alaina. She sort of stood out onstage out of the twenty people around her. All the people onstage were like between the ages of eight and forty-five. I took a seat in the pews. The choir director was telling them about the different octaves that they should sing in. The choir director sort of seemed feminine. His mannerisms were like those of a thirty-year-old lady. He had a high-pitched voice, and he swished whenever he walked. I assumed that he was gay. He sort of resembled Blair Underwood in his younger days.

"Alright, everybody, let's take a ten-minute break," he said. Everybody walked off of the stage. Alaina walked up to me.

"I'm so happy to see that you made it."

"Hey, I'm a man of my word."

"Well, come on. Let me introduce you to Michael, my choir director." She grabbed my hand and led me over to the choir director. "Hey, Michael, this is my friend Shamrock whom I was telling you about."

He hugged me. I was caught a little off guard by it. "It's so nice to meet you, Shamrock. Alaina told me that you're very talented."

"Well, I wouldn't say all of that," I replied shyly.

"He's very modest," Alaina said.

"He's also handsome," the choir director added. I didn't know whether he was coming on to me or this was just his personality. "Where are you from, Shamrock?"

"I'm from Lakeside," I replied.

He made a shocked face. "Oh my God!" he gasped. "I guess the Lord places his talent everywhere in this world."

"Did he know that he just offended me?" I thought.

"Well, why don't you just get up onstage and bless us with what the Lord has given you?"

"I don't know. I haven't sung in ages," I said.

"It's aight, baby. Trust me . . . when you get up there, it's all going to come out naturally. Doesn't the church want to hear this young man's singing ability?" He said to the audience of those who were sitting in the pews. Their attention was on us three. All of them said yes. I hadn't planned on singing tonight. I couldn't believe that he had put me on the spot like that.

"Come on, Shamrock. If it makes you feel better, I'll go up there with you," Alaina said.

I took a deep breath. "Alright. I'll do it," I replied. Alaina and I walked up onto the stage.

"What do you two want to sing?" Michael asked. Alaina looked at me. "His Eye Is on the Sparrow" was the first song that popped into my head.

"'His Eye Is on the Sparrow,'" I replied.

"Hallelujah. That's a good choice!" Michael said. I was beginning to see that Michael was really animated. He handed Alaina and me two microphones. "The stage is yours," He said. He went and sat behind the piano and began to play the tune.

I started off singing the first line. "Why should I feel discouraged?"

Alaina sung the second, "Why should the shadows come?"

We took turns singing lines. The church got riled up. There were a lot of hallelujahs and amens being shouted from the audience. It felt like old times again being up there. Michael was right. The words just came naturally. Alaina was also a wonderful singer. She hit the notes at the right moments. We both ended the song in high notes. The audience by then was out of their seats clapping and praising the Lord. I looked over at Michael. I saw tears in his eyes.

The music stopped. Michael stepped onto the stage. He took the microphone from me and put his arm around my neck. "Now, congregation, that is how you praise the Lord. This church hasn't seen singing like that in a long time. Can I get an amen?"

The people in the audience said amen.

"Young man, you are really talented," he said. "Alaina, you were spectacular, too."

Alaina blushed. "I haven't gotten shaken up like that from a performance in along time," he said. "You know, it would be a blessing if you two could bless the service tomorrow with a duet. How about it?" He looked at us.

"It's alright with me," Alaina said.

All eyes were then on me. I hadn't planned on this. I admit though—it did feel good being up in front of the crowd again. I didn't have anything to lose. "It's fine by me," I said.

"Praise the Lord!" Michael yelled. Michael was starting to grow on me. I was starting to like him. "Well, what I want you two to do is get together and go over what y'all want to sing."

"Alright," we replied.

"As for the rest of the choir, y'all break is up. Everybody get back on stage. We have some work to do."

Alaina and I walked off of the stage and sat down on a pew in the back of the church. "You were wonderful," Alaina told me.

"Thank you. You were, too," I replied. She stared into my eyes. "Is there something on my face?" I asked.

"No," she replied.

"It's just that you resemble my . . ." She was interrupted in mid sentence by a familiar voice. I looked up and saw a very familiar face staring right into my eyes. "Thank you, Ms. Sally," Alaina replied.

It was Ms. Sally, the old lady who owned the barbeque restaurant whose purse I'd snatched. I was lost for words. I sort of sat there frozen.

"Shamrock, this is Ms. Sally. She's one of our ushers." Ms. Sally smiled at me.

"Nice to meet you ma'am," I said.

"You know, young man, you look familiar. Where have I seen you before?"

Once again I was lost for words. "I can't recall," I replied. "I hope that God will forgive me for lying inside of church," I thought. This situation was very awkward. I looked at my watch. "You know, it is getting kind of late, and my Aunt Jesse is working late tonight. I have to go look after my little brother."

I had told another lie in church. I rose up. "Alright then, Shamrock. Well, I'm going to call you tonight so that we can discuss the song that we're going to sing tomorrow."

"Alright," I replied.

"It was nice meeting you, Ms. Sally," I said. She smiled at me. I walked out of the church. "What are the odds of this happening?" I thought as I walked to my car. I got into my car and drove home. When I got back to the Shaw, I saw Sno-Cone's yellow Caprice sitting in the parking lot. I got out of the car and walked over to it. Sno-Cone and Ras were sitting in it. I started to get angry. I thought I told Sno-Cone not to bring this dude around me anymore. If he said anything smart to me, there would be some problems.

I approached the driver's side where Sno-Cone was sitting. "What's up, Sno-Cone?"

"What's up, dog?" he replied. I didn't speak to Ras. "Hey, I was just coming over here to tell you that Doodle's graduation party is this upcoming Tuesday. We're having it at Airport Park, the gigantic park over on Cooper Road."

"I know where it's at," I said.

"Well, I'll be by your pad to pick you up at 9:30 straight. You better be ready."

"Alright," I replied.

"Your ex-girlfriend Keisha's going to be there, too," he said jokingly. I didn't find it funny. I walked toward my building as he pulled out of the parking lot.

# CHAPTER 9

## Alaina's Point of View

Candy and Brandy had once again invited me to a place where I was uncomfortable going, but like always, I agreed to go. We were on our way to a frat party that they got invited to by Milky-Way and Doodle. Being around a bunch of drunk, college guys didn't really interest me much. "Wow, I can't believe we're on our way to our first frat party."

Candy said, "Do you think that there's going to be a lot of guys there?"

"Of course," Brandy responded.

"I just hope nothing stupid goes down," I said.

"Here you go thinking negatively again. Alaina, could you just for once loosen up and have some fun?" Brandy stated.

"Yeah whatever," I replied.

We drove until we got to Maguire's University Campus. We showed the guard at the gate our ID cards, and he let us through. The campus was packed that night. It was hectic. I was starting to get flashbacks of the strip last week. "Man, there's a lot of people here tonight," I said. We followed the line of cars to a gigantic two-story house all the way in the back.

Somehow, we squeezed into a parking spot. We got out of the car and headed toward the entrance of the house. There were cars and people everywhere. There was a group of people on the front lawn playing football in their underwear. There were six girls against six guys. The guys were hiking the football. The quarterback threw the football to a guy who was tackled by a petite girl.

"Got you!" she yelled.

"Put on some clothes," Brandy playfully yelled. We went into the house. The music was blasting, and there was barely any walking room. People were dancing and jumping around on couches. A chugging session caught my attention in the corner. A group of guys was chugging beer through a long tube from a keg. All the other guys were cheering on one of them.

"Hey, there's Doodle," I said spotting him in the crowd of people. We walked over to him.

"What's up, superstar?" Candy said, tapping him on the back. He turned around.

"Hey!" he yelled. He gave Candy a hug. I could tell that he was high from the way that he was talking. "I thought you guys weren't going to show up."

Brandy started to look around. "Hey, where's your friend?" she asked.

"Oh, he's over there by the deejay booth." We spotted him behind the booth talking to the deejay. Doodle walked over and grabbed Milky-Way.

"Hello, ladies," Milky-Way said hugging the three of us

I looked into Milky-Way's eyes. Milky-Way was the most handsome guy I'd ever seen. I was sort of jealous that he and Brandy were talking. Brandy whispered something in his ear.

They both laughed. The song that was playing suddenly turned off.

"Alright, everybody, we're about to give y'all something special. The Pussycat dancers are about to bless y'all with a dance." Everybody started to laugh.

"Who are the Pussycat dancers?" I asked.

"Oh you'll see," Doodle said laughing. Just then four guys busted from out of nowhere, prancing to the middle of the room. They were dressed in daisy dukes and shirts that didn't cover their navels. I could easily tell that they were gay. Everyone was now quiet, staring at them with interest.

"Alright, Pussycat dancers, are you ready?" the group's leader said. He had dreadlocks and was the skinniest out of all of them.

"Meow," the group responded in unison. Everybody laughed. The deejay put on R&B singer Kelis's song "Milkshake." They began to dance. They began to dance very feminine, shaking their hips and wiggling in womanly manners. They weren't that bad. All the guys in the room were laughing. Most of the women were dancing along with them. They ended their dancing with a split.

Everybody clapped. "Well, they were entertaining," I thought.

"They were great," Brandy said.

"Hey, let me introduce y'all to them." Doodle called them over. "Hey, Pussycats, let me introduce y'all to my friends."

"Hey, how y'all doing?" We all shook hands. "Girl, your hair is so pretty," the leader told me.

"Thank you."

"Brandy, Candy, and Alaina, these are the Pussycat dancers."

"Y'all did really great out there," Brandy said.

"Thanks, Shawty," their leader said. "I'm Jessie and this is Bobby, Dreka, and Corey."

"Nice to meet y'all," I said.

"So, what are y'all doing after the show?" Jessie asked.

"Probably chilling and getting a bite to eat," Doodle said. "Y'all wanna come?"

"For sure," Bobby said.

"Alright then. We're probably going to meet up at eight o'clock outside."

"Alright then."

"Milky-Way, why are you so quiet tonight?" Bobby asked.

"I'm just chilling, bro," he replied.

"Milky-Way, you so crazy," he replied jokingly.

"Well, see y'all at eight then," they said as they walked off.

The lights dimmed. "Alright, party people, I'm going to slow it down with some 'Brokenhearted' by Brandy." Doodle and Milky-Way took Candy and Brandy on the floor. I took a seat on a sofa by the wall. I hated being a third party. It kind of made me feel left out.

I pulled out my phone and checked my text messages. I didn't have any new ones. I sat back in the chair. Brandy's "Brokenhearted" was one of my all-time favorite songs. "How I knew about a broken heart," I thought. This sofa chair sure was comfortable. I closed my eyes and began to drift.

I didn't know how long that I'd been asleep, but I was awakened by loud yelling. I opened my eyes. I looked at my watch. It was 10:30. I'd been asleep for two hours. I looked at the ruckus coming from the right side of me. A big crowd had gathered.

"Well, folk, if you going to do something, then do it." I could see that a fight was about to break out. I got up to look for Candy and Brandy. I ran outside to see if they were at the car.

They weren't. I saw Bobby, one of the dancers, standing by a bright red Camaro. I walked up to him. "Bobby, have you seen Candy and Brandy?"

"No, Shawty, I haven't seen any of them."

I went back into the house. I pushed my way through the crowd of people. The two guys were still up in each other's faces. Candy and Brandy had to be amongst this crowd somewhere. "Maybe they're upstairs," I thought. I made my way upstairs. I walked down the hallway. Maybe they were in one of these rooms. I spotted a door that was cracked at the other end of the hallway. I walked to it. I thought I could hear a voice coming from the room. I peeked in.

What I saw I wasn't prepared to see. I thought my eyes were playing tricks on me. I saw Milky-Way and Jessie, the dancer from the Pussycats, passionately kissing each other. I stared at them in disbelief. I didn't know that Milky-Way was gay or bisexual, or whatever. As if something or someone told Milky-Way to look up, he peered toward me. He pushed Jessie away from him. "Hey, trick, come here," he yelled.

I ran down the other end of the hallway and back downstairs. I was now confused. I pushed my way through the crowd. I bumped into Candy. "Candy, I've been looking all over for you."

"Oh, you've finally woken up, sleepyhead."

I could tell that she was tipsy. "Candy, you're drunk."

"Girl, no, I'm not," she said.

"Where's Brandy? We're fixin to leave."

"She's over there with Doodle." I saw Brandy sitting in Doodle's lap on a sofa. I grabbed Candy's hand, and we walked over to them.

"Hey, Brandy, I'm ready to leave."

"Girl, why? We've just gotten here." I could tell that she was drunk too.

"I'm ready to go," I said. "Where's the keys?"

She reached into her pocket and gave them to me.

"Alright, well go." She continued to flirt with Doodle.

I grabbed her arm and softly yanked her off of Doodle's lap. "Brandy, let's go." She looked into my eyes and saw that I was serious.

"Doodle, I'm going to give you a call tonight. My girl is tripping right now."

"Alright then, Shawty." They hugged and then we left.

"Alaina, why are you tripping?" We got into car.

"Candy and Brandy, y'all aren't going to believe this, but I just saw Milky-Way and Jessie kissing upstairs." They both looked at me with their mouths open.

"Girl, stop lying. Milky-Way is not gay."

"Well, he and Jessie must be very good friends then," I replied.

Candy burst out laughing. "I know Shawty wasn't that pretty for nothing."

"I can't believe it," Brandy said.

Just then Milky-Way came busting out of the front door of the house running toward the car. "Hey, Alaina, I need to talk to you for a second," he yelled. I cranked up the car and sped out. I looked at him through the rear-view mirror.

"I'm a little nervous, Alaina." I said as I looked into the crowd. The church was packed this afternoon—maybe because it was the first Sunday of the month. Alaina and I were sitting next to each other on stage, along with the other twenty choir members. The preacher was just getting ready to wrap up his sermon, and Alaina and I were about to go on.

"I'm nervous, too, but we're singing for the Lord," Alaina said.

I spotted my Aunt Jesse sitting next to Kix in the second row. I told her that I would be performing at a friend's church, and even though she didn't go to this church, she said she wouldn't miss it for the world. She used to come see me sing when Mom was alive. The preacher finished his sermon. The preacher was surprisingly young.

He looked to be around thirty-two to thirty-five years of age. Most preachers that I've seen were like in their forties and fifties. He was a slender young man, too. I hadn't seen too many black preachers who were skinny. They'd usually have big bellies.

"Now that the Lord's message has been given, we're going to be blessed by two young talented people, whom the Lord has blessed with the gift of song." He looked back at the choir. That was our cue. We got up and stepped up to the microphones. We'd agree to sing "Jesus Is Real," one of my all-time favorite gospel songs. Michael began to play the tune on his piano.

"Put your hands in the air if you believe the Lord is real," Alaina said into the microphone.

Almost everybody in the church rose to his or her feet. The choir started off the song singing "Jesus is real. I know the Lord is real to me."

Alaina started off the first verse. "Sometimes I feel him in my bones; nowhere to go, Jesus comes along, and he makes me strong." The audience all began to cheer. There were some people dancing in the aisle. When the choir finished singing the chorus, I began the second line. "Sometimes when I'm feeling down; no one around, Jesus is a friend." My nervousness started to go away when I saw my Aunt Jesse with her hands in the air. Kix was up and clapping, too.

We traded lines throughout the whole song, and everybody in the church loved it. The preacher was sitting down in his chair with his eyes closed, grooving to the music. I ended the song on a high note. "Jesus is real." The crowd clapped. The preacher stood up and approached the microphone.

"Hallelujah! Jesus is indeed real because we can see it in these two beautiful young people and our lovely choir. That was amazing," he said. "Now, the church all knows our lovely Alaina, but many of y'all may not be familiar with this young man.

"Young man, how about you come up to the podium and introduce yourself." He moved out of the way to let me step behind the podium.

I cleared my throat. "Well, my name is Shamrock, and I'm from Lakeside. I was invited to come here by y'all's talented members, Alaina and Michael." Michael raised his hand up in the air and smiled so he could take his credit. Some of the church members laughed.

"I came here with my lovely Aunt Jesse and my little brother Kix." They stood up. "I haven't been to church in awhile, but being here, I've been motivated to start going back. I also thank you all for inviting me here."

The audience said amen. I went to sit down. The preacher stepped back up to the podium.

"Amen, bless your heart. We're happy to have you here," the preacher said. "It's a blessing to see you come back to the house of the Lord. If only more young people thought the same way . . . can I get an amen, church?"

The church said amen. After he finished talking, he dismissed church. I stepped down from the stage. Everybody came up to me and started giving me hugs and handshakes. Alaina came and kissed me on the cheek. I was a little caught off guard by it.

"You were amazing," she said.

"You were, too," I said.

"Hey, do you want to hang out today? Maybe we could go see a movie or something," she asked.

"Yeah, that would be great; I just have to go and get out of these church clothes," I replied.

"Cool. I'll give you a call in like two hours."

"Alright," I replied. I went to my Aunt Jesse.

"Antron, you were great! If your mother was alive, she'd be so proud of you."

"Thanks, Aunt Jesse," I replied.

"Yeah, you were awesome, big bro," Kix told me. I rubbed his head.

We started walking toward the exit. Ms. Sally, the usher, was standing near the door as we were walking toward it. She smiled as we approached her. I was starting to feel a little uneasy. "You were awesome, young man," she told me as she hugged me.

"Thank you ma'am," I replied, trying to get away from her.

She grabbed my hand, as I was about to walk out of the door. She reached over and whispered in my ear, "I forgive you."

I stared at her. I didn't know what to say. She smiled at me. "How did she know?" I thought. "I . . . I . . ." I started stuttering.

She softly shushed me, putting her finger to her lips. "It's alright," she said. She motioned me toward the door because she had to greet more people as they left. I exited out the entrance. I was flabbergasted. She knew it was me and didn't have me arrested. I assumed that by her forgiving me that God had forgiven me, too. I looked up into the sky.

"Thank you, God." I whispered. I got into the jeep with Aunt Jesse and Kix, and we drove off.

# Chapter 10

## Alaina's Point of View

I was just about to end another day's work at Edge Me Ups barbershop. In another hour and a half, I'd be getting off of work. I began to sweep around my area. I'd probably call up Candy and Brandy tonight and ask them if they'd like to go see a movie. As I swept and thought about what movie that I was going to go see, I felt a tap on my back. I turned around to face a young guy whom I'd never seen before.

"Yes," I responded.

"Yeah, I was wondering if you could hook me and my homeboys up with a cut."

"Sure," I replied. "Where's your homeboys?" I asked. He motioned outside. There were like twelve guys walking toward the entrance. I looked at them.

"A friend referred us to you. He said that you cut the best fade in town."

I felt confused for a second. "Who could have referred them to me?" And then it came to me. I smiled. "Well, your friend was right," I replied. "Sit down." He took a seat in the chair.

All of his friends came into the shop.

"Girl, looks like you're going to be pulling some overtime," one of the barbers told me.

I smiled.

"Looks like I am," I said.

# CHAPTER 11

## Ras's Point of View

Once again, I was hanging out with these young dudes again, but Sno-Cone begged me to come to his friend Doodle's graduation party. It was a Friday night, and we were on our way to pick up Shamrock from his house. We pulled into the driveway, and he was already standing in the parking lot. I was riding in the front seat, and I refused to give it up today. He walked up to the car. He rolled his eyes when he noticed that I was on the passenger side. This time he didn't even argue. He hopped into the backseat with Milky-Way.

"What's up, dog?" Sno-Cone greeted him.

"What's up, man?" he replied. He gave Milky-Way a handshake. He didn't say anything to me, as I expected.

"Is Doodle already at the park or something?" Shamrock asked.

"Yeah," Sno-Cone replied.

"Hey, Shamrock, there's going to be a lot of girls at this party," Milky-Way said.

"Man, here you go talking about girls again," Shamrock said playfully. "None of them are going to be looking at you; they're going to be looking at me anyways," Shamrock said.

Milky-Way burst out laughing. "That's a good one, bro."

"Hey, Sno-Cone, you might have to take me home early because I have to go pick up my car from my sister. Is that cool?" I asked.

"Yeah, it's straight," Sno-Cone replied.

"Man, no one should have to miss a party to take you home, cuz," Shamrock said. I turned around and looked at him.

"What?" I asked.

"Man, don't even bother wasting your time with him, man," Sno-Cone said.

I refrained from saying anything. Shamrock was this close to me going off on him. We finally made it to Airport Park. The park was a pretty good turn out. There were at least close to 600 people there. Sno-Cone parked his car on a basketball court across the street, overlooking the whole park.

"Man, there's a lot of people here tonight," I said.

"The more, the merrier." Sno-Cone replied. We walked across the street to the party. Shamrock pulled out his phone.

"Hey, Doodle just texted me, saying he's over by the deejay table." We made our way over to it. We found Doodle at a park bench with four people playing dominoes.

"Domino!" he yelled as he slammed the domino unto the table. We walked over to him.

"Man, Doodle, why you over here fronting like you know how to play dominoes?" Shamrock said teasingly. He rose up from his seat and gave Shamrock and Sno-Cone a hug. He gave me a handshake.

"You finally made it," Sno-Cone said.

"Yeah, I finally made it, dog. I don't have to put up with those teachers and Principal Jenkins anymore."

"Shamrock, your girl Keisha was looking for you earlier," Doodle told him.

"Where is she?"

Doodle pointed toward the direction where she was. Shamrock walked over to find her.

"Man, y'all friend is whipped," I said. I sat down on the bench next to Doodle. "I got next game." I spotted Shamrock and Keisha hugging. His friend was cute. She wasn't my type though. I also spotted her brother and his crew standing not to far from them. I sure didn't feel like getting in a fight with them today. I just wanted to relax. I tapped Sno-Cone. "Hey, looks like our friends are here," I said as I pointed toward Keisha's brother and his crew.

"Man, don't even worry about them."

# CHAPTER 12

## Shamrock's Point of View

"You finally made it out, huh?" I said to Keisha as I smiled at her.

"Yeah, I finally made it."

"I heard you got valedictorian, too."

"Yeah, I got valedictorian also." We went to go sit at an unoccupied picnic table.

"I've been thinking about what you've said about me trying to do something with my life."

"That's great."

"Yeah, I got this friend whom I've been talking to, and they've sort of convinced me to do better with my life."

She looked at me, confused. "What friend have you been talking to?"

"Oh, just some friend that I met a couple of weeks ago."

"Is it a girl?"

I looked at her, confused. "Yeah, why does that matter?" I asked.

"Oh nothing," she replied. "It's just that I've been telling you this for a while, and you've always shrugged me off. But now that some other girl has told you something, you take heed."

I looked at her. "Well, my new friend and I have a lot in common. You're never around anymore now that you hang out with your new friend, Semaj." She had nothing to say. "It seems to me like you're a little jealous." She looked at me. "Maybe I am a little," she replied.

"How's your friend been doing anyways?"

"He's been doing alright. He's always busy with schoolwork, so I never see him that much."

Just then, the deejay turned on Earth Wind and Fire's song "Reasons." "This is my jam right here," I said. "Does the valedictorian care to dance with a lil old thug like me?" I asked playfully.

"Sure," she replied. We got up and started slow dancing in the middle of everyone. We sat there and danced for a few minutes. The moon and the stars had come out. My cell phone vibrated in my pocket. I took it out and looked at the number. It was Alaina.

"Hey, give me a couple minutes," I told Keisha.

"Alright."

I answered the phone. "Hello."

"Hey, Shamrock."

"What's up, Alaina? Hey, I'm gonna call you back in like thirty seconds. I'm about to walk to my friend's car because there's too much noise out here."

"Alright," she replied. I hung up the phone and walked across the street to Sno-Cone's car. I hopped in the passenger seat. Ras had left his cell phone in the front seat. It was ringing. "How can you be so careless and forget your cell phone?" I said aloud. I dialed Alaina's number. She picked up after the second ring.

"What's up?" I said to her.

"Hey, how you doing?" she replied.

"I'm good now that you've called."

"It sounds like you're at a party or something."

"Yeah, I'm at my homegirl and homeboy's graduation party. It is jam-packed out here."

"Well, I don't want you to get into any trouble out there."

"Oh, don't worry—in a little while I am about to call it a night. Besides if I get into trouble, I'm not going to be able to get into college."

"What are you talking about?"

"Well, I'm taking the ACT test tomorrow. I'm going to try to apply for this community college in my neighborhood."

"Shamrock, that's great," she replied. "You're starting to let the Lord work with you."

"Yeah, but it was you whom God sent to me. If it wasn't for you, I wouldn't even be thinking of college. I'm glad that you came up to me and said hi for whatever reason that night at Lakeside Strip."

There was silence on the other end of the phone. "Alaina, are you still there?"

"Shamrock, I want to thank you for what you did the other day. I know it was you who referred all of those guys to me. Your friends said that they're going to start coming to me on a regular basis now. I actually have regular customers now."

"Oh, it was nothing. I was doing them a favor. I can't keep the best barber in the city a secret." There was once again silence on the other end of the phone. "Alaina, you got to stop with all of these brief pauses," I said semi-seriously.

"I'm sorry. It's just that sometimes I get caught up in your eyes and the sound of your voice. You remind me a lot of my older brother, Rashawn."

"I do?" I asked.

"Yeah you do. I've tried telling you that a few times. Both of you guys are headstrong people, yet gentle."

"Well, like the saying goes, we all have a twin somewhere," I said.

"You're right. Speaking of my older brother, I need to get in touch with him. His son is crying for him." I heard a baby crying in the background. "Hey, Shamrock, I'm going to call you back. I got to take care of my nephew."

"Alright," I replied. I hung up. "Alaina sure is nice," I thought. Ras's phone rang again.

I didn't even bother to look at it. I looked across the street at everyone at the party. Milky-Way was talking to some girl, as usual. Sno-Cone was at the picnic table playing dominoes. Keisha was talking to one of her male friends. I looked around for Ras. I found him standing by a truck. Keisha's brothers and his crew were walking slowly toward him. "Looks like someone is about to get it," I whispered to myself. Everybody noticed the commotion going on and started to go over and investigate.

Ras's phone continued to ring. It was starting to annoy me. Keisha's brother now had pulled out a pistol. "Oh man," I said aloud. Ras had his hands out, pleading with them to calm down. "He deserves it," I said. "How can he just come in and barge in on somebody's crew? He's not even from Georgia; he's from North Carolina." I continued to look across the street at them. I started to think back in hindsight. Alaina said her family moved here from

North Carolina. I thought about all of the times when she would just pause and stare at me . . . when she tried to tell me that I reminded me of her brother, but was always interrupted. She said her brother was into the streets very hard.

I thought about how Sno-Cone said Ras and I fought like brothers, and how Alaina said her brother and I were both headstrong. I looked at Ras's phone ringing. I picked it up. I stared at it anxiously. I pressed the send button . . . put the receiver to my ear . . . .

"Hello," I said. There was an awkward silence on the other end of the phone.

"Shamrock, is this you?" a very familiar voice answered.

"Alaina, Ras is your brother?" I asked.

"Yeah, but why are you answering his . . . ?"

I dropped the phone and ran across the street toward Ras and the crowd. Tazarus now had the gun pointed toward Ras. Keisha was grabbing his arm, pleading with him to put down the gun. I ran faster toward them.

"Don't shoot!" I yelled. Ras ran toward him whenever he turned around to look toward me. I ran in front of Ras. Just as I was running in front of him, Tazarus saw Ras and me advancing toward him and let off four shots. A sharp pain pierced through my chest as I fell to the ground.

My vision was very blurry. All I could see was people running in every direction. Keisha knelt down and cradled my head in her arms. "Shamrock, it's going to be alright," she said sobbing.

"Somebody call an ambulance," I heard Milky-Way yell. It was suddenly starting to get difficult for me to breathe.

"Shamrock, don't die on me, man!" I heard Sno-Cone yell. My eyes uncontrollably rolled back into my head, and then from there . . . total darkness.

# Chapter 13

## Alaina's Point of View

It had been three days since the shooting, and I hadn't gotten any sleep. All I could think about was Shamrock. I was in the elevator heading up to the fifth floor to visit Shamrock. He'd been in a coma since the shooting. Doctors said there was a fifty-fifty chance he'd pull out of it. One of his lungs was damaged. I made it to his room, 516. I stepped into the room. Shamrock was lying on a bed. He looked peaceful.

A nurse was standing by his bed checking his IV. "How's he doing?" I asked.

"He's still hanging in there. He's a very strong young man."

"Yeah, I know that," I replied. She left the room. I went to stand by his bed. I gently squeezed his arm. I'd heard that, when people are in comas, they sometimes can hear what you are saying. "Shamrock, I miss you," I said to him. "You know, everybody's been asking about you at church. We're all praying for you. You have to get well so you can serenade me some more. I'll never forget that night as long as I live.

"You're such a beautiful person, Shamrock." I silently began to cry. "You know I've been thinking about what you said—you know, about how God has us all floating down here kind of like we're freestyling, and it's up to us to make the best out of life. I think you're right. There was reason that I was drawn to you at the strip that night.

"You looked like a man who was destined to be great. You're talented, handsome, and charismatic. What person wouldn't be drawn to you? I even wrote a poem dedicated to you."

I pulled a piece of notebook paper that I'd written the poem on.

*Is it fate or coincidence when two people cross each other's path?*
*I can't seem to figure it out.*
*I'll let you do the math.*

*There we were, two people*
*Going down life's highway.*
*You were going your way.*
*I was going my way.*

*And then by chance we bumped*
*Into each other coincidentally.*
*And it just so happened*
*That we connected mentally.*

*So is it coincidence or is it fate*
*That brings together two soul mates?*

I paused. Tears began to stream down my face.

*Maybe it's both.*

"Get well, Shamrock. You have to stick around so God can tell you what direction to point me in." I put the poem back in my purse. I kissed Shamrock on his forehead and walked out of the room. I took the elevator down to the first floor and walked out of the hospital to my car. I got into the car. I checked my cell phone. I had two missed calls from my psychiatrist, Ms. Collins. I had a session that day at three o'clock.

I turned on the radio. Earth Wind and Fire's "Would You Mind" came unto the radio. It was the song that was playing the night Shamrock and I hung out at Johnson's Gorge. I turned up the volume. I started thinking about that night on the Gorge when Shamrock and I were discussing life and about how my parents died in the accident. I remembered telling him how I guilty that I felt and the advice that he'd given me. "Why don't you tell your parents how you feel?" he had said. I thought about what he said. Then out of nowhere I had an epiphany. I understood what Shamrock was trying to tell me. I never gave him a chance to explain himself. I put the car in drive and sped out of the hospital parking lot.

It was a nice and sunny Saturday afternoon in North Carolina. I was at Chandler's Cemetery standing in front of the two tombstones of my parents, John and Flora Harris. It was my first time ever visiting their gravesite. I bent down and put flowers beside each of their tombstones. "Momma and Daddy, it's your little girl Alaina. I'm sorry it took me fifteen years to come see you. I've just been having trouble coping with the loss of you two. Not a single day has gone by when I haven't thought about you two.

"I miss you two so much. LaNeisha, Rashawn, and Vanessa have been doing alright. I still hold onto the lessons that you've all taught me." I began to weep. "Momma and Daddy, I just want to tell you that I'm so sorry. I never wanted anything to happen to you two. I'd give anything to bring you two back. I love you two so much." I closed my eyes and felt the cool wind blowing on my face. I exhaled. "I'm finally free," I whispered. "I'm cured," I said loudly. All the guilt that I'd let build up for fifteen years had disappeared just like that. I turned around and motioned for Rashawn, LaNeisha, and Vanessa to come to me.

They'd all agreed to come with me. It was the first time in years that I'd seen LaNeisha and Rashawn together. They approached me, and we all had a group hug in front of our parents' gravesite. Rashawn gave LaNeisha and Vanessa a kiss on the cheek. It was a beautiful sight. I stood there and took it all in.

"Thanks Shamrock," I said aloud.

The End.